Sleeping Beauty

PUFFIN BOOKS

Published by the Penguin Group
Penguin Books Ltd, 80 Strand, London WC2R 0RL, England
Penguin Putnam Inc., 375 Hudson Street, New York, New York 10014, USA
Penguin Books Australia Ltd, 250 Camberwell Road, Camberwell, Victoria 3124, Australia
Penguin Books Canada Ltd, 10 Alcorn Avenue, Toronto, Ontario, Canada M4V 3B2
Penguin Books India (P) Ltd, 11 Community Centre, Panchsheel Park, New Delhi – 110 017, India
Penguin Books (NZ) Ltd, Cnr Rosedale and Airborne Roads, Albany, Auckland, New Zealand
Penguin Books (South Africa) (Pty) Ltd, 24 Sturdee Avenue, Rosebank 2196, South Africa

Penguin Books Ltd, Registered Offices: 80 Strand, London WC2R 0RL, England

www.penguin.com

First published 2003
4

Set in 16/25 Cochin

Made and printed in England by Clays Ltd, St Ives plc

British Library Cataloguing in Publication Data
A CIP catalogue record for this book is available from the British Library

ISBN 0–141–31644–6

Sleeping Beauty

Narinder Dhami

PUFFIN BOOKS

Contents

Chapter One

'Long live Princess Aurora! Long live Princess Aurora!'

A large, colourful procession was winding its way through the town towards the castle. Soldiers in armour trotted along on horseback, followed by trumpeters and jugglers. Banners and flags fluttered in the breeze, and the townsfolk wore their best and brightest clothes.

There was great excitement throughout

the land because at last a baby princess had been born. King Stefan and his Queen had longed for a child for many years and finally their wish had been granted. Now everyone had gathered to celebrate the arrival of little Princess Aurora.

Inside the castle, the throne room was teeming with people. The King and Queen were seated on their thrones, smiling proudly at their daughter, who lay sleeping peacefully in her cradle. Even a sudden blast of trumpets didn't wake her up.

A herald stepped forward and unrolled a large scroll. 'May I present Their Royal Highnesses King Hubert and Prince Phillip,' he announced loudly.

King Stefan's face lit up. 'Ah, my old friend,' he murmured to the Queen.

King Hubert bustled into the throne room, followed by his young son, and embraced King Stefan. The two kings were very different – Hubert was as short and round as Stefan was tall and thin – but they had been good friends for many years.

'We have a special gift for your new daughter.' King Hubert beamed. He handed a golden box to his son and gently pushed him towards Aurora's cradle.

Phillip peered in at the baby and pulled a face. Babies are boring, he thought to himself.

King Hubert watched his son bending

over Aurora's cradle and smiled at King Stefan. Phillip didn't know, but both kings had already decided that, when their children were old enough, they would be married. The announcement was to be made this very day...

There was another fanfare of trumpets. Everyone turned to look at a bright, golden sunbeam shining into the castle courtyard. Three glowing sparkles floated in the beam of light. Slowly they changed shape, one by one turning into three plump little fairies.

'Their most Honoured Excellencies, the three good fairies,' announced the herald. 'Mistress Flora, Mistress Fauna and Mistress Merryweather.'

The three fairies wore exactly the same

long dresses, cloaks and pointed hats, but Flora's were orange, Fauna's green and Merryweather's blue. Beaming all over their kind, round faces, they bobbed through the air towards the cradle.

'Oh, the little darling,' Merryweather whispered, peeping in at the baby.

Flora turned to the King and Queen. 'Your Majesties,' she said with a smile, 'each of us the child may bless, with a single gift, no more, no less.' She lifted her wand. 'Little Princess, my gift will be the gift of beauty.' She waved her wand and a shower of flowers fell softly into the cradle.

Then Fauna stepped forward. 'Tiny Princess,' she said, 'my gift will be the gift of song.' With that, sparkling lights drifted down from her wand and into the cradle.

'Sweet Princess,' Merryweather began, 'my gift will be the –'

But the third fairy did not get any further. Suddenly a huge gust of wind howled around the throne room, almost knocking her over. The doors flew open, setting all the banners dancing wildly. Everyone gasped as the hall grew dark. Jagged streaks of silver lightning were followed by a terrifyingly loud crack of thunder.

Green flames began to flicker up from the floor. Higher and higher they grew, twisting and turning, until they formed themselves into a formidable shape. A tall, slender woman dressed in flowing black robes stood before them. She wore a horned headdress and carried a slim cane topped with a golden globe. The woman was very beautiful, but her face was cold and hard and pale. Her presence sent an icy chill through the room.

The three fairies looked anxiously at each other.

'Why, it's Maleficent!' Fauna whispered.

'What does she want here?' Merryweather asked with a frown.

Chapter Two

As everyone stood in silence, a large black raven flew in through the open doors. It came to rest on top of Maleficent's cane.

'Well,' Maleficent purred softly, glancing around the throne room, 'quite a glittering party, King Stefan. Everyone seems to be here. Royalty, nobility...' Her gaze fell on the three fairies standing by the cradle. 'Even the rabble!'

'Ohhh!' Merryweather gasped crossly.

She tried to fly at Maleficent, but Flora pulled her back.

'I really felt quite distressed at not receiving an invitation myself,' Maleficent went on silkily.

'You weren't wanted!' snapped Merryweather.

Maleficent put a hand to her throat, pretending to be embarrassed. 'Not wanted!' she cried. 'Oh dear. What an awkward situation.' There was a tense silence as she stroked the raven's sleek black feathers. 'I had hoped that it was due to some oversight. But in that case, I'd best be on my way.'

'And you're not offended, Your Excellency?' the Queen asked.

A smile twisted Maleficent's mouth.

'Why, no, Your Majesty. And to show that I bear no ill will, I too shall bestow a gift on the child.'

The three fairies gasped in alarm, drawing closer to the cradle.

'Listen well, all of you!' Maleficent proclaimed, striking her cane on the ground. 'The Princess will indeed grow in grace and beauty, and be beloved of all who know her ...'

The King took the Queen's hand. They both looked pale and fearful.

'But before the sun sets on her sixteenth birthday,' Maleficent continued, 'she will prick her finger on the spindle of a spinning wheel and DIE!'

'Oh no!' the Queen cried. She ran over to the cradle and picked up the baby.

Pointing at Maleficent, King Stefan shouted furiously to the guards, 'Seize that creature!'

However, Maleficent just laughed. 'Stand back, you fools,' she cried, raising her arms.

The sleeves of her robe billowed around her. Lightning flashed and thunder roared. Seconds later Maleficent was swallowed up in a mass of leaping green flames and she vanished from sight.

The throne room was suddenly eerily silent, except for the faint echoes of her evil laughter.

Chapter Three

'Don't despair, Your Majesties,' cried Flora. 'Merryweather still has her gift to give.'

The King looked hopeful. 'Then she can undo this curse?'

'Oh no, Sire,' Merryweather replied.

'Maleficent's powers are far too great,' said Flora.

'But she can help,' Fauna added.

Merryweather waved her wand over the baby's cradle. 'Sweet Princess, if through this wicked witch's trick, a spindle should your finger prick, not in death but just in sleep, this fateful prophecy you'll keep. And from this slumber you'll awake, when true love's kiss the spell shall break.'

Merryweather had done the best she could, but the King and Queen were still terrified that Maleficent's evil spell would harm their beloved daughter. So that very day, King Stefan ordered that every spinning wheel in the kingdom should be brought to the palace and burnt. A huge bonfire blazed in the castle courtyard as the spinning wheels were set alight.

'A bonfire won't stop Maleficent,' remarked Merryweather gloomily.

The three fairies were in the empty

throne room, watching the orange flames leaping up into the night sky.

'Of course not,' Flora agreed.

'Oh, I'd like to turn that Maleficent into a fat old toad!' Merryweather muttered.

'Now, dear,' said Flora, 'you know our magic doesn't work that way. We can bring only joy and happiness.'

'Well, it would make me happy!' Merryweather replied.

'There must be a way,' Flora went on. Then a smile spread across her face. 'Yes! I believe there is!'

'What?' asked Fauna.

'Ssh!' Flora waved her wand, shrinking herself down. 'Even walls have ears. Follow me.'

Flora flew across the room towards the

table where the Princess's christening gifts lay. One of them was a little gold box with two doors. Flora flew into the box, followed by Fauna and Merryweather. The doors closed and the key locked behind them.

'Now, let's see,' Flora said to herself, as Fauna and Merryweather waited impatiently. 'The woodcutter's cottage. No one lives there any more. The King and Queen won't like it, of course. But when we explain it's the only way ...'

'Explain what?' asked Merryweather.

'About the three peasant women who will be looking after a baby, deep in the heart of the forest,' Flora replied.

Fauna and Merryweather looked puzzled.

'Who are they?' Merryweather wanted to know.

As Flora waved her wand, Fauna and Merryweather's fairy outfits vanished and they were dressed in simple peasant clothes.

'Why, it's us!' Fauna cried. 'You mean we'll take care of the baby?'

'If humans can do it, so can we,' Flora said firmly.

'And we'll have our magic to help us,' Merryweather added.

'No!' Flora shook her head. 'No magic! Then Maleficent will never suspect what's going on.' She took Fauna's wand. 'And let's get rid of those wings too.'

Meanwhile, Merryweather had backed away, looking worried. 'You mean live like humans for sixteen years?' she gasped, trying to hang on to her wand as Flora took it. 'But we've never done anything without magic!'

'Oh, we'll all pitch in,' Flora assured her. 'Now, we must tell Their Majesties at once!'

As Flora had guessed, the King and Queen were very upset at the thought of their baby being taken away from them. But they also knew that it was the best way of stopping Maleficent's evil curse from coming true.

So late that night, three peasant women stole out of the castle and into the forest. One of them carried a baby in her arms.

The King and Queen watched sadly from the balcony as Flora, Fauna, Merryweather and Princess Aurora disappeared into the night.

Chapter Four

'It's incredible!' cried Maleficent as she stalked around the throne room of her palace on top of the Forbidden Mountain. Her face was pale with fury as she turned on her guards. 'Sixteen years! Sixteen years have passed and not a trace of Princess Aurora anywhere!'

The guards blinked sheepishly.

'She can't have vanished into thin air!' Maleficent snapped. 'Are you sure you've searched everywhere?'

'Yes, everywhere,' mumbled their leader. 'The town, the forest, the mountains. And all the cradles.'

Maleficent turned to face him, her robes swirling around her. 'Cradles?' she repeated.

The leader nodded.

The raven was sitting on the arm of Maleficent's throne. She reached out and stroked the bird's throat. 'Did you hear that, my pet?' she said softly. 'All these years, sixteen long years, they've been looking for –' she glared at the guards – 'a BABY!'

There was a clap of thunder and the guards shrank back.

'Fools!' Maleficent was furious. 'Idiots!' She aimed lightning bolts at the guards, who ran off, tumbling down the stairs in their efforts to get away. Then, sitting down on her throne, she turned and spoke to the raven at her hand. 'You are my last hope. Go and look for a girl of sixteen with hair of sunshine gold.'

The raven flew off through the open window.

'And do not fail me,' Maleficent called after him.

Deep in the heart of the forest was a small woodcutter's cottage. The three fairies had lived here for the past sixteen years, caring for Princess Aurora, whom they had named Briar Rose. Today was her sixteenth birthday.

'We'll make a dress,' Flora decided.

'And a cake,' said Fauna.

'But how are we going to get Briar Rose out of the house?' Merryweather wanted to know.

'What are you three dears up to?' Briar Rose asked, coming downstairs. She was tall, slender and beautiful, with long golden hair.

'We want you to go and pick some berries,' said Merryweather, handing Briar Rose a basket.

'I picked berries yesterday,' Briar Rose began.

'We need more, dear,' said Flora quickly. 'But don't go too far.'

'And don't speak to strangers,' Fauna added.

Smiling, Briar Rose went off into the

forest. As soon as she had gone, Flora opened a trunk and took out a length of pink material, while Fauna hurried into the kitchen.

'I'll get the wands,' said Merryweather, heading for the stairs.

'No magic!' Flora reminded her. 'I'll make the dress.'

'And I'll make the cake,' said Fauna.

Merryweather stared at them. 'But you can't sew and you've never cooked!'

'It's simple,' Flora laughed. 'You can be the dummy, Merryweather!'

Merryweather stood on a stool and Flora wrapped the material round her before she began cutting.

'But it's pink,' Merryweather grumbled.

'I wanted it to be blue.' Then she sighed and tears came to her eyes. 'After today, we won't have any Briar Rose. She'll be a princess again.'

'We've had her for sixteen years,' Flora reminded her, but she too suddenly felt sad.

Meanwhile, Fauna was following the recipe in a cookery book. 'Three cups of flour,' she muttered. 'Two eggs ...' And she threw the eggs in, shells and all.

'This looks awful!' Merryweather complained, staring down at the material wrapped round her.

'That's because it's on you, dear,' Flora retorted.

Fauna slapped some icing and candles on top of the cake mixture and stepped back to admire it. 'Well, what do you think?' she asked. 'Oops!' The icing was sliding on to the floor. 'It'll be better when it's baked.'

'I think we've had enough of this nonsense,' Merryweather said in disgust. 'I'm going to get those wands!' And she stomped off upstairs.

'Fauna, close all the windows,' Flora said as Merryweather bounced back downstairs with the wands. 'We can't be too careful. Fauna, you take care of the cake, Merryweather, you clean the room and I'll make the dress.'

The three fairies waved their wands. Immediately, the bucket, mop and broom sprang into action and began to clean the cottage. Flour, eggs and milk poured themselves into a bowl and began to mix together. Scissors danced about, cutting the pink material into the shape of a beautiful dress.

Merryweather pulled a face. 'Make it blue!' she insisted, flourishing her wand.

'No, pink!' Flora argued, waving her own wand.

Blue and pink sparks flew back and forth as the material changed colour every few seconds. There were so many sparks, some of them flew up the chimney.

Maleficent's raven was soaring high in the sky overhead. He spotted the magical sparks whirling out of the chimney straight away and flew down to take a look.

Chapter Five

Briar Rose walked through the forest, humming to herself and swinging her basket. As she passed by, birds sang in the trees, squirrels peered at her with bright eyes and rabbits popped their heads out of their holes. They were so accustomed to Briar Rose that they weren't scared of her at all.

'I wonder, if my heart keeps singing, will my song go winging, to someone who'll find me?' As Briar Rose sang while

'We have a special gift for your daughter.' King Hubert beamed.

'My gift will be the gift of song.' Fauna waved her wand.

*'I too shall bestow a gift on the child,' Maleficent said with a tw
smile.*

*The King and Queen watched sadly as the three fairies and Prin
Aurora disappeared into the night.*

'We want you to go and pick some berries,' said
Merryweather.

'I know you, I walked with you once upon a dream,'
Briar Rose sang.

h had the strangest feeling they had met before.

'Touch the spindle!' Maleficent's voice echoed around the room.

'You fools!' Maleficent hissed. 'Here's your precious Princess!'

...ge black dragon breathing yellow fire stood in Maleficent's place.

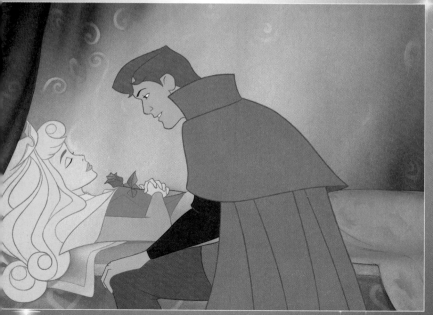

The Prince bent over the bed and gently kissed her.

'I – I don't understand!' King Hubert stammere

she picked berries, her voice echoed through the trees, sweet and clear.

Not far away, Prince Phillip was riding through the forest. Like Briar Rose, he was no longer a child. He was now a tall, handsome young man. He pulled his horse up sharply when he heard the faint, sweet sound and smiled.

'You hear that, Samson?' he said, patting the horse. 'Let's go and find out who it is.'

Briar Rose put her basket down and sighed. 'Oh dear, why do they still treat me like a child?'

'Who-oo?' said an owl, swooping down from the tree.

'My aunts, Flora, Fauna and Merryweather,' Briar Rose explained.

'They never want me to meet anyone.'
She smiled dreamily. 'But in fact I have
met someone. In my dreams. A prince...'

She began to twirl round on the grass,
singing, 'I know you, I walked with you
once upon a dream...'

Suddenly someone was behind her,
gently taking her hands and joining in
the song.

'Oh!' Briar Rose spun round. She saw
a handsome, finely dressed young man.

'Sorry.' Prince Phillip smiled. 'I didn't
mean to frighten you.'

As they stared at each other, both had
the strangest feeling that they had met
somewhere before.

'What's your name?' Phillip asked.

'It's – it's –' Briar Rose stammered,

blushing. 'Oh no, I can't!' And she turned and ran.

'But when will I see you again?' Phillip called anxiously.

'This evening.' Briar Rose smiled to herself as she hurried away. 'At the cottage in the glen.'

Briar Rose wandered home in a happy dream, thinking about the handsome man she had just met. Flora, Fauna and Merryweather were waiting for her. The cottage was spotless, the cake looked delicious and the blue dress was beautiful.

'Happy birthday!' the three fairies chorused.

'Oh!' Briar Rose gasped. 'This is the

happiest day of my life. Everything's so wonderful.' She smiled at the three fairies. 'Just wait until you meet him!' She began to sing. 'Once upon a dream ...'

'Him?' Fauna repeated, staring at Briar Rose. 'She's in love!'

'This is terrible!' Flora sighed.

'Why?' Briar Rose looked puzzled.

Fauna took her hands. 'You're already engaged,' she said gently.

'Since the day you were born,' Merryweather added.

'To Prince Phillip, dear,' Fauna explained. Briar Rose's eyes widened. 'But how could I marry a prince?' she asked. 'I'd have to be —'

'A princess,' Merryweather broke in.

'And you are,' Fauna told her.

'Princess Aurora,' said Flora.

Briar Rose looked from one fairy to the other. She couldn't believe what they were saying. None of them noticed Maleficent's raven perched near the open door.

'Tonight we're taking you back to your father, King Stefan,' Flora went on. 'And I'm afraid you must never see that young man again.'

Tears welled up in Briar Rose's eyes. 'Oh no!'

She ran upstairs, leaving the three fairies staring sadly at each other.

Noiselessly, the raven slipped away and flew with haste back to Maleficent's palace.

Chapter Six

The whole kingdom was waiting joyfully for the Princess to return home, but no one was more excited than the King and Queen, who hadn't seen their beloved daughter for sixteen years. King Stefan and Phillip's father, King Hubert, were waiting impatiently for the three fairies to bring Aurora to the castle.

'No sign of her yet,' muttered King Stefan, who was staring anxiously out of the window towards the forest.

'Tonight we toast the future!' Hubert said happily, raising his wine glass. 'Our children will marry and our kingdoms will be united!'

'His Royal Highness, Prince Phillip!' announced a herald, as the young man galloped into the castle courtyard on his horse.

'Phillip!' King Hubert jumped to his feet and dashed down the steps to greet his son. 'Hurry, boy. Go and get changed. You can't meet your future bride looking like that!'

'But I have met her, Father,' cried Phillip, laughing. He grabbed King Hubert and danced around with him. 'Once upon a dream!'

'Now, what's all this dream nonsense?'

his father blustered, straightening his crown.

'It wasn't a dream, Father,' Phillip said, his eyes shining. 'I really did meet her.'

King Hubert looked amazed. 'You met the Princess Aurora?'

'I said I met the girl I am going to marry,' replied Phillip happily. 'I don't know who she is. A peasant girl, maybe.'

'A peasant girl?' King Hubert gasped in horror. 'No, Phillip, you can't do this to me! You're a prince and you're going to marry a princess!'

'You're living in the past, Father,' Phillip said firmly. 'This is the fourteenth century and I'm going to marry the girl I love!' With that, he jumped on Samson's back and galloped off.

'Phillip, stop!' King Hubert called. He shook his head sadly. 'How will I ever tell Stefan?'

Meanwhile, Flora, Fauna and Merryweather were leading Briar Rose through the forest. Not a soul was about as they made their way across the castle courtyard and into the castle. The three fairies took her to a lavishly decorated bedroom, where a fire had been lit to welcome them.

Flora sat Briar Rose down at the dressing table. 'This one last gift, dear child, for thee,' she said softly, 'the symbol of thy royalty.'

The fairies waved their wands. A gold crown studded with sparkling jewels appeared and Flora placed it gently on the Princess's head. Briar Rose stared at herself in the mirror and began to cry.

Flora ushered Fauna and Merryweather out of the room. 'Let her have a few moments to herself,' she whispered.

Left alone, Briar Rose sobbed bitterly. She did not notice that the fire was burning brighter, or that wisps of smoke were rising higher and higher into the air.

The smoke faded, and the evil face and figure of Maleficent glowed briefly at the back of the fireplace. Then she too faded into a bright green wisp of smoke.

Briar Rose looked up and saw the emerald smoke floating in the air. She stood as if in a trance and moved towards it. Strange, haunting music played softly as she headed straight for the fireplace.

Outside, the three fairies were talking in low voices.

'Oh, I don't see why she has to marry a prince!' Merryweather was muttering.

'Listen,' Flora whispered as she heard the music drifting out from the room. 'It's Maleficent!'

Pale with terror, the fairies burst into the room. They were just in time to see the brick wall at the back of the fireplace open up and Briar Rose disappear behind it.

'Rose!' they called, dashing forward to stop her. But it was too late. Just as they reached the opening, the bricks reappeared.

'Rose!' called out Flora, once the fairies had finally moved the wall aside with their magic. 'Rose, where are you?'

Her eyes wide and dazed, Briar Rose followed the glowing green smoke up a circular stairway. At the top of the steps stood an open door and she went inside. The wisp of smoke was hovering in the centre of the room. As she walked towards it, it curled and stretched and formed itself into a spinning wheel. At the top of the wheel was a very long, sharp spindle.

'Rose!' Flora, Fauna and Merryweather were hurrying up the stairs. 'Don't touch anything!'

'Touch the spindle!' Maleficent's voice echoed round the room. 'Touch it, I say!' Briar Rose reached out slowly towards the spindle . . .

The three fairies rushed into the room and gasped as Maleficent loomed over them.

'You fools!' she hissed. 'Thinking you could defeat me!' She pulled her robes aside. 'Well, here's your precious Princess!'

Chapter Seven

Briar Rose was lying on the floor, her golden hair spread around her. She looked pale and still.

'Oh, Rose!' the three fairies wailed, as Maleficent disappeared in a burst of flames and smoke, her sinister laugh echoing after her.

Meanwhile, the King and Queen were waiting impatiently for their daughter to arrive. The main hall was full of people who had come from all over the kingdom to celebrate. The only person who wasn't happy was King Hubert. He tugged at his friend's arm.

'Er – Stefan, I've got something to tell you,' he muttered, wondering how he was going to break the bad news about Phillip.

'Ssh!' King Stefan hissed, as a herald stepped forward.

'The sun has set,' the herald announced. 'Make ready to welcome the Princess!'

Everyone cheered and colourful fireworks began to explode in the dark sky.

The three fairies had gently placed the sleeping Aurora on the bed and now looked tearfully at one another.

'Poor King Stefan and the Queen,' Fauna said softly.

'They'll be heartbroken when they find out,' Merryweather sniffed.

Flora brushed away a tear. 'They're not going to,' she decided. 'We'll put them all to sleep until Rose awakens!'

Quickly, Flora, Fauna and Merryweather made themselves tiny and flew off around the castle, scattering magic sleep-dust. They began with the guards, who yawned and fell asleep where they stood. Then they moved into the banqueting hall, where people were feasting, and in a few moments everyone was sound asleep there too.

Flora flew over to King Hubert and

King Stefan.

'I've – er – just been talking to Phillip,' Hubert said awkwardly, yawning hugely as Flora scattered her sleep-dust, 'and he's fallen in love with some peasant girl …'

But King Stefan was already asleep and King Hubert's eyes were beginning to droop as well.

Flora's face lit up. 'A peasant girl!' she gasped, and flew straight over to King Hubert. 'Where did he meet her?'

The King opened one eye. 'Once upon a dream,' he yawned, and then he began to snore.

'Rose! Prince Phillip!' Flora cried excitedly. She hurried back to the others. 'We've got to go to the cottage!'

*

As they flew out of the castle and returned to the forest, Flora explained what she had discovered. When the fairies reached the cottage, they were expecting to see Prince Phillip waiting for Briar Rose, but there was no sign of him. The cottage was dark and empty.

'Look!' Flora had spotted something lying on the floor. She swooped down and picked it up. It was a hat with a feather in it. 'Prince Phillip was here.'

'Maleficent!' Merryweather gasped. 'She's got the Prince!'

'At the Forbidden Mountain,' Flora said, with dread in her voice.

'But we can't go there!' Fauna cried.

'We can and we must!' Flora announced firmly.

Chapter Eight

Maleficent's palace stood, dark and gloomy, on top of the tall, black mountain. Flora, Fauna and Merryweather hid behind a rock and peered out, checking for guards. Then they bobbed their way over to the drawbridge.

Suddenly a guard appeared and they whisked themselves back out of sight once more. Next they made themselves into small specks and this time they managed to fly into the castle without being spotted.

The fairies landed on a window-ledge and peeped down into the room. The guards were dancing around a large, blazing fire, while Maleficent sat on her throne, stroking the raven.

'What a pity Prince Phillip can't be here to join in the celebrations,' she purred. 'We must go to the dungeon and cheer him up.'

She rose and walked over to a flight of steps, the raven flying along beside her. Unseen, Flora, Fauna and Merryweather followed. At the bottom of the stairs, in a dark, damp dungeon, sat Prince Phillip, chained to the wall. He looked cold and miserable.

'Oh, come now, Prince Phillip.' Maleficent smiled wickedly. 'Why so sad? In the topmost tower of King Stefan's palace lies the Princess Aurora.' Her smile widened. 'The very same peasant girl you met in the forest! She lies in an ageless sleep. And in one hundred years' time you will be free to leave this dungeon, a grey-haired old man, and ride off to waken your love with love's first kiss!'

Her laughter echoed around the dungeon as Prince Phillip sprang angrily to his feet, straining to break free from his chains.

'You –' Merryweather tried to fly at Maleficent, but the others held her back. The raven turned his head curiously, his bright eyes peering through the darkness.

'A most gratifying day,' Maleficent said with satisfaction, as she and the raven left the dungeon.

Wasting no time, the three fairies flew down from the window-ledge. Prince Phillip's eyes widened in amazement as they shot up to their normal size.

'Ssh!' Flora tapped the shackles on his arms and they fell away. 'No time to explain!'

Fauna did the same to the chains on his ankles, while Merryweather peeked out of the door, checking for guards.

'Arm thyself with this enchanted shield of virtue and this mighty sword of truth.' Flora waved her wand, and a shield and a sword appeared in the Prince's hands. 'Now come, we must hurry.'

They all rushed from the dungeon, but only to come face to face with the raven, which was flying down the stairs.

Chapter Nine

'Caw! Caw!' the raven squawked
furiously, and flew back up the stairs to
fetch the guards.

Prince Phillip turned and ran the other
way, and the fairies bobbed along behind
him. They found another staircase and
dashed up it as the guards came running
towards them. At the top of the stairs
was a window. The fairies flew through it
and Prince Phillip jumped after them
down into the courtyard. Samson, who

was chained too, heard his master and whinnied loudly.

'Phillip,' Flora called, as the guards began to hurl boulders from the window, 'watch out!' She waved her wand, turning the boulders into harmless bubbles.

As Merryweather set about burning through Samson's chains with magic, the guards began firing arrows at them. Flora waved her wand again and the arrows turned into flowers that simply fell to the ground.

Prince Phillip urged Samson forward as the raven flapped overhead. The horse raced towards the drawbridge, just as the guards started pouring boiling oil in their path. But Flora was ready with her wand again and turned the oil into a dazzling rainbow.

The raven whirled round and, calling loudly, flew up to the throne room to warn Maleficent. Merryweather followed him. The determined little fairy chased him round and round the tower and, with one whisk of her wand, turned him to stone. Then she flew back to join the others.

'Silence!' Maleficent thundered, stalking out of the tower room. 'Tell those fools to –' Her eyes widened as she realized that her raven had been turned to stone. 'NO!'

Now the castle drawbridge was rising higher and higher as Prince Phillip galloped desperately along it.

'Watch out, Phillip!' Fauna cried.

All three fairies waved their wands, helping Samson to make the giant leap from the rising drawbridge to the rocks beyond.

Furiously, Maleficent rushed to the top of the tower and lifted her cane, her robes billowing in the wind. She hurled a lightning bolt at a stone arch as Phillip rode through it, sheltering beneath his shield. Another lightning bolt hit the rocky ridge and the path crumbled away. Samson and Phillip slid down the side of the cliff, the fairies flying anxiously above them.

'A forest of thorns shall be his tomb,' Maleficent cried, staring at King Stefan's palace in the distance, 'borne through the skies on a fog of doom. Now go with a curse and serve me well. Round Stefan's castle, cast my spell.'

Lightning bolts immediately struck the castle and a great wall of thick thorny branches began to grow, twining upwards to a great height and blocking the Prince's path.

Phillip rode forward, his face determined. He began to hack his way through the thorns as Samson whinnied with fright. Soon he was panting and his hands were cut and bruised, but he did not stop until he had forced a way through to the palace.

Maleficent stared in horror. 'No!' she cried, and instantly vanished in a whirl of purple and gold sparks. A second later flames flared in front of Prince Phillip, and Samson reared up in terror as Maleficent appeared.

'Now you shall deal with me, O Prince,' Maleficent hissed, 'and all the powers of HELL!'

The flames leapt higher and Maleficent shot upwards, becoming taller, her shape changing. Seconds later a huge black dragon breathing yellow fire stood in her place.

As the fairies watched, horrified, the dragon spat a stream of flames at Phillip. He fell off his horse and backed away towards the edge of the cliff. Another blast sent him tumbling over, even closer to the edge. Desperately, he lashed out with his sword at the dragon's head as its long, sharp teeth snapped and snarled. The next blast knocked the shield from the Prince's grasp.

'Ha ha ha!' Maleficent's evil laughter echoed through the flames as the dragon moved in for the kill.

Quickly, the three fairies touched the tip of the Prince's sword with fairy dust.

'Now sword of truth, fly swift and sure,' Flora cried, 'that evil die and good endure!'

Prince Phillip pulled back his arm and hurled the sword with every bit of strength he possessed. It buried itself deep in the dragon's chest. With a cry, the wounded creature stumbled forward, then plunged over the edge to the bottom of the cliff.

Chapter Ten

Prince Phillip hurried through the castle courtyard. He noticed the people standing around, sleeping where they stood, as he headed towards the tower room where Aurora lay.

The three fairies watched happily as he bent over the bed and gently kissed her. Her eyes opened slowly and she smiled as she recognized the Prince. There was no need for any words.

In the rest of the castle, everyone else

began to wake up as well. King Stefan and his Queen opened their eyes. So did King Hubert.

'Now, Hubert, you were saying?' Stefan turned to his friend.

'Well...' King Hubert looked embarrassed. 'To come to the point, my son Phillip says he's going to marry –'

There was a blast of trumpets. As everyone turned, Phillip and Aurora came down the stairs smiling, hand in hand.

'It's Aurora!' King Stefan cried in delight. 'She's here!'

King Hubert rubbed his eyes in disbelief as Aurora ran into her mother's arms. Up on the balcony, the three fairies smiled at each other, tears of happiness in their eyes.

'I – I don't understand!' King Hubert stammered.

Aurora smiled and kissed him on the cheek, and then, as the music began, she danced off across the floor with her Prince.

'Oh, I love happy endings!' Fauna sobbed.

'So do I,' Flora agreed. Then she frowned as she noticed Aurora's blue dress. 'Pink!' she whispered, lifting her wand.

'No, blue!' Merryweather replied, changing the dress back again, as the Prince and Aurora danced on, knowing that now they would live happily ever after.